The Child's World of
THANKFULNESS

Library of Congress Cataloging in Publication Data

McDonnell, Janet, 1962–
Thankfulness / Janet McDonnell
p.   cm.
Originally published: c1988
Summary: Describes the feeling we call thankfulness and the things that
can make us thankful.
ISBN 1-56766-295-1
1. Gratitude—Juvenile literature.   [1. Gratitude.]
I. Title.
BJ1533.G8M37   1988
                              88-2657
                              CIP
                              AC

The Child's World of
THANKFULNESS

By Janet McDonnell • Illustrated by Mechelle Ann

THE CHILD'S WORLD

What is thankfulness?

Thankfulness is what you feel when you have someone to sing you a song when you can't sleep.

You can feel thankful for hot chocolate and a blanket on a cold, snowy day, or for icy lemonade and a shower on a hot, dry day.

When you visit your grandma and she has made your favorite dinner, you feel thankful.

When it's been raining all morning and you want to go on a picnic, and you finally see the sun, you feel thankful.

And when your mom's flowers are all dying because the ground is hard and dry, you feel thankful when it finally starts to rain.

You can be thankful for a baby-sitter who reads all your favorite stories.

And thankful is how you might feel when your dad finds your favorite car that you lost a long time ago.

When you have a sore throat and a stuffy nose and your mom brings you ice-cream and sits with you, you are thankful.

You can be thankful for big things, like a park down the street where you can play, or for small things, like a chocolate-chip cookie.

Sometimes it's easy to forget how thankful you are for something, such as a healthy body, or a family that loves you.

If you look very carefully, you will find something to be thankful for every day.

Thankfulness is feeling happy for what you have. When you are thankful, you feel warm and glad and lucky, all at the same time.

What are you thankful for today?